Everyone thinks the Porker
children are perfect. Even Miss Wolf,
the new librarian at their school.
One day she discovers how truly bad
they are, and the Porkers
are in for a shock.

MORE BITES TO SINK YOUR TEETH INTO!

LET IT RIP!
Archimede Fusillo
Illustrated by Stephen Michael King

LUKE AND LULU
Bruce Davis
Illustrated by Chantal Stewart

THE GUTLESS GLADIATOR
Margaret Clark
Illustrated by Terry Denton

Miss Wolf and the Porkers

These little Porkers are in for a shock!

Bill Condon

Illustrated by Caroline Magerl

RUNNING PRESS
KIDS
PHILADELPHIA·LONDON

For Susan Bryant and Liana Steptoe, and the teachers
and children of St. Mary's Eagle Vale,
New South Wales *B.C.*
For Maureen, Bill, Duncan, and Jennifer *C.M.*

Copyright © 2001 Bill Condon
Illustrations © 2001 Caroline Magerl

First published by Penguin Books Australia, 2001

Printed in China

9   8   7   6   5   4   3   2   1
Digit on the right indicates the number of this printing

Library of Congress Control Number: 2005935359

ISBN-13: 978-0-7624-2649-2
ISBN-10: 0-7624-2649-7

Original design by David Altheim and Ruth Grüner, Penguin Design Studio.
Additional design for this edition by Frances J. Soo Ping Chow

Typography: Blur, MetaPlus, and New Century School Book

This book may be ordered by mail from the publisher.
Please include $2.50 for postage and handling.
But try your bookstore first!

This edition published by Running Press Kids, an imprint of
Running Press Book Publishers
125 South Twenty-Second Street
Philadelphia, Pennsylvania 19103-4399

Visit us on the web!
www.runningpress.com

Ages 7–10
Grades 2–4

ONE

This is the tale of the Porker Kids and a nice librarian called Miss Wolf. We'll meet her soon, but first, the Porkers...

The kids' names were Rails, Dan, and Shorty. Rails was short for Raelene, Dan was short for Dandruff, and Shorty was just short.

Each of the Porkers had curly red hair, happy smiles, and more freckles than you'd find on a freckle farm.

They looked like any other kids,

but they had a special talent. The Porkers were World Champions when it came to sucking up to teachers.

They carried their teachers' books.

They cleaned their car windshields.

They gave them apples (with hardly any worms in them).

And they wrote sweet little poems for them, like this:

Our teachers are so cute and kind.

They teach us very well.

They might look a bit like zombies

But they hardly ever smell.

The teachers at Mount Barker School were certain that Rails, Dan, and Shorty were perfect angels.

Conk!

How perfectly wrong they were.

Behind the Porkers' syrupy smiles lay a dim, dark secret. Sucking up to teachers was not their only talent. The Porkers were masterminds at Being Bad—and getting away with it, every time.

Here's some of the vile deeds they got up to in just one quarter.

Rails crept into the assembly hall and put a whoopee cushion under the Vice Principal's seat.

Dan released a mob of mice that terrorized the cafeteria ladies.

And, in the most daring, rude and crude crime of all, Shorty drew

a colored picture of Principal Kidney's naked pink bottom and hung it from the school flagpole.

Everyone at Mount Barker, except the angelic Porkers, was questioned about that, even Principal Kidney's mother. (Who else would know his bottom was pink?)

Luckily, Mrs. Kidney had a sound alibi. She was color-blind, and she couldn't draw bottoms.

"Who could the villains be?" asked the teachers. "Not the Porkers, that's for sure. They're far too nice to be naughty."

"Sucked in!" sniggered the Porkers.

TWO

One day a new teacher arrived at assembly. She was a tiny woman, whose chubby-cheeked face was rosy red. She had large, sticking-out ears, and long, gleaming black hair. When the wind blew, her hair flew straight out behind her, so that it looked like Count Dracula's cape.

"Hello, children," she said in a warm and friendly voice. "I'm Miss Wolf, the new school librarian."

She hesitated, as if expecting the

audience to burst into applause, throw
money, and rush for her autograph.

The only sounds she heard were
yawns and groans of boredom.

Principal Kidney stepped forward
to shake her hand. "Now don't worry,
children," he said. "Even though

our new librarian's name is Miss
Wolf, she's not the kind of wolf who
eats children."

Miss Wolf looked horrified. "Eat
children? Me? Never! No, no, no.
I promise I won't, even if their library
books come back late!"

"It was just a little joke," said Principal Kidney.

"Oh . . . was it?"

"Yes, Miss Wolf. Of course it was."

The hall was eerily silent.

Miss Wolf was suddenly aware
that everyone was staring at her very
strangely. She felt uncomfortable
and silly and *extremely* embarrassed.
Her face turned bright red. Then
the silence was broken by her
nervous giggles.

"Oh, silly, silly me," she said, just
seconds before the giggles grew into
a giant belly laugh. Soon her belly
jiggled about like a barrel of
ping-pong balls in an earthquake.

The other teachers, who only
moments before had looked like
a bunch of undertakers at their own
funeral, began laughing too.

Even Principal Kidney joined in, and he hadn't laughed since the day he caught the seagull that stole his wig!

Miss Wolf's laugh had turned a disaster into triumph. She grinned with pleasure.

"But seriously," she continued, "I hope to see every one of you children at the library. You'll have a jolly good time—because libraries are fun! Let's all say it together . . ."

Two hundred bored children dragged out the words as if saying them for the millionth time,

"LIBRARIES ARE FUN."

The Porkers winked at each
other, their piggy eyes gleaming
with nastiness.

"We'll have lots of fun at the
library, all right," whispered Rails.

13

"But it won't be from reading boring books."

Shorty and Dan slapped hands, up high and down low.

"We've never driven a librarian crazy before," said Shorty.

Dan licked his lips. "I can hardly wait."

THREE

The Porkers didn't care much for books. There were too many words in them. But that's not what they told Miss Wolf.

"We absolutely adore books," said Rails. She smiled adorably. "Even ones without pictures."

Shorty hugged a dictionary to his chest as if it was his favorite teddy bear. "I'd rather read a book than watch television or play computer games."

"I read two books every day. Not the same two, either," said Dan.

Miss Wolf hopped about excitedly and clapped her hands.

"How enchanting it is to meet young people with a love of literature," she gushed. "If you like, you can be my special library monitors."

"What a pushover!" thought the Porkers. "Now to have some fun."

All through lunchtime the Porkers worked quietly in the library. They only stopped to smile at Miss Wolf, who smiled back radiantly.

Then things started going wrong.

Children swarmed in front of

the library desk, demanding Miss
Wolf's attention.

"The last page of *A Hundred Fun
Things To Do With Fleas* is torn out,"
lamented Kylie. "Now I won't be able
to finish the necklace I'm making."

"I was reading *The Case of the Clawed Hand* when a hand reached out from behind a shelf and grabbed my neck," complained Jacob.

"Yuck!" cried Mandy. "There are worms in this book."

"Eek!" screeched Belinda.
"Bookworms!"

As Miss Wolf frantically attempted to get her library back in order, she spied two fat rats playing hide and seek on the Food and Nutrition shelf.

"Rats!" wailed Richard.

"Eek!" said Belinda, who was rapidly becoming fond of that word.

There was a stampede out of the library.

"Come back," pleaded Miss Wolf.

"No!" yelled the children.

"Never, ever!"

Miss Wolf flopped into a chair, too flabbergasted to speak. Meanwhile, the ever-helpful Porkers rounded up the rats and deposited the worms safely out on the lawn. They even managed to find the missing page of *A Hundred Fun Things To Do With Fleas.*

The Porkers gathered around Miss Wolf, looking as innocent as babies.

"Thank you so much for your help, children," she said.

"We had fun doing it," said Rails. "Um—fun helping you, I mean."

Miss Wolf nodded. "Of course, dear child. I know precisely what you mean."

"I've never seen anything like that before," said Shorty as he repaired the torn page.

"If you ask me," said Dan, "someone's playing tricks on you, Miss Wolf."

Rails shook her head, oh, so sadly. "Who would do such a rotten thing?"

"I don't know," Dan replied. "But they'll be in big trouble from me if I find out."

A tear trickled down Miss Wolf's cheek. "How lucky I am to have the lovely Porker children looking after me."

FOUR

The next day the Porkers found a
blue tongue lizard. Just to see what
would happen, they left it inside the
library's bathroom.

Shorty rubbed his hands together
in anticipation. "This will be good,"
he said.

Three Porker heads peeked out
from behind the picture-book shelf
as Miss Wolf visited the bathroom.

They expected her to run out
screaming. Instead, she ambled out

of the bathroom, stroking the lizard, which was curled up comfortably on her shoulder.

"Poor Lizzie got a bit lost, I'm afraid," she said. "I almost squashed her."

"So you're not afraid of lizards, then?" asked Dan.

"Heavens, no," declared Miss Wolf. "I'm a country girl. Lizards, spiders, snakes—they don't bother me at all."

The Porkers ached with disappointment.

"But cockroaches—now that's a different story," she said, making

a face. "I can't stand those dreadful prehistoric pests. They make my skin crawl."

"How interesting," said Shorty.

"How wonderful," said Rails softly.

The following day Miss Wolf read a pop-up book to a class of tiny tots.

Directly in front of her, the Porkers watched out of peepholes they'd made in the Geography shelf.

As Miss Wolf flipped a page, two huge black cockroaches popped out of the pop-up book.

The class squealed as the cockroaches scampered up Miss Wolf's bare arm.

The Porkers fell about laughing.

Out of the library tore the tiny tots, as if being chased by Godzilla and his big hairy brother.

Miss Wolf's skin *might* have been crawling, but there was no way of telling that from her face. If anything, she seemed calm.

She didn't scream, nor did she run. She merely watched the cockroaches intently as they frolicked on her arm.

"I say she faints," said Shorty.

"I say she throws up," said Rails.

"Hey," said Dan enthusiastically, "maybe she'll do both!"

Miss Wolf did neither.

Instead, she swept up the cockroaches in her hand, and gobbled them up!

"Oh, yuck!" said Rails and Shorty.

"I'm going to throw up," said Dan. And he did.

"We saw that, Miss," said Rails, emerging from her hideout.

"That's right," said Shorty.
"You're not scared of cockroaches. You
eat them!"

Dan, looking distinctly green
around the gills, trailed slowly behind
the others. "That was really gross,"
he said. "I threw up."

Miss Wolf didn't hear them. She stared straight ahead, her eyes glazed.

"Are you all right?" asked Rails. She snapped her fingers. "Miss Wolf!"

Miss Wolf blinked, then shook her head. "What happened?"

"I threw up," said Dan.

"Oh, you poor child," said kindly Miss Wolf. "Was it something you ate?"

"No. It was something *you* ate."

"Cockroaches!" shouted Rails and Shorty.

"Oh yes, I remember now," said Miss Wolf with a shiver. "It must have been the stress."

"The stress?" said Rails.

Miss Wolf glanced around to check that they were alone.

She motioned the Porkers closer.

"You won't tell anyone this, will you?"

"No," said the Porkers.

"Sometimes, when I get very, very stressed, I do the strangest things."

As she spoke, Miss Wolf's eyes appeared to become larger than before. And so did her mouth.

"What sort of things?" asked Dan.

"I . . . I become—no! I can't tell you. It's too horrid."

"That's not fair! Tell us! Please!"

"I must spare you. You'll have nightmares."

"We love nightmares," said Rails.

"My answer is no, children. Just protect me from stress. Otherwise, who knows what dastardly things may happen."

FIVE

The Porkers weren't a bit scared by
what Miss Wolf said. However, they
didn't want to make her suspicious,
so for the next few weeks, all returned
to normal at the library.

There were no more lizards or
cockroaches, rats or worms. No more
torn books, or creepy hands that
throttled unsuspecting readers.

As word got around that the library
was safe again, the children returned.
Miss Wolf personally welcomed every

child. She gave each of them an I Love
Libraries badge, and a creamy
chocolate that she'd made herself.

Before long, the library was the
most popular place in school.

Even the teachers came to visit. (Though the kids suspected they were just after the chocolates.)

Miss Wolf bubbled over with happiness.

"Oh, I do enjoy being a librarian," she trilled. "It is such deeeelightful fun!"

All this time the Porkers had been on their best behavior.

They helped Miss Wolf cover books, they returned borrowed books to their shelves, they even made her a cup of tea if she was tired.

When Miss Wolf asked if they had any ideas for a library display, the Porkers came up with a dozen.

"We only need two displays, dears," said Miss Wolf.

"No worries, Miss," said the Porkers.

They gave up their lunchtimes to create dazzling displays: a pyramid made of books, and a book rainbow!

Miss Wolf clutched at her heart when she saw their work. "My goodness me!" she exclaimed. "Such creativity, such kindness. Without a doubt, you are the best children in the world."

Once they were alone, the Porkers strutted proudly about, congratulating themselves. But not for their good deeds.

"We are such tricky tricksters!" whooped Shorty.

"We're the kings of cunning!" said Dan.

"Kings *and* queen," corrected Rails. "We've got Wolfie eating out of our hands. She'll never suspect us."

Soon the Porkers had devised another sneaky trick to play on Miss Wolf. Not some tired old trick, either. They had never thought up a better or a sneakier plan!

SIX

The next morning the Porkers waited outside the library when Miss Wolf arrived for work.

"It's only 8:15," she said. "Why are you so early for school, children?"

"We came to help you before class starts," said Rails with a smile.

"We'll help again at lunchtime," offered Dan.

"After school, too," said Shorty.

"That's so terribly kind of you," Miss Wolf said. "I can't accept, of course.

You've done enough for me already."

From behind her back, Rails
produced a bouquet that they'd picked
on their way to school.

Miss Wolf beamed with happiness.
"Onion weed!" she said. "How lovely."

"A weed?" said Shorty. "We didn't know that. Honest!"

"Please don't apologize, dear child. It is a beautiful thought, and of all the weeds, the onion variety is truly my favorite."

The Porkers stood at the doorway, looking up at Miss Wolf like lost puppies.

"You're so uncommonly cute," she said.

Then came the words that they'd been hoping to hear.

"I wish there was something I could do to repay you for all your kindness."

"As a matter of fact," said Rails, trying not to sound too eager, "you *could* do us a favor."

"Wonderful!" declared Miss Wolf. "Tell me what it is. If it's possible, I'll be glad to help."

"It's our grandma who we really

want to help," said Dan. "She loves
books, almost as much as we do,
but it's too far for her to walk to the
public library."

"She's almost a hundred years old,"
explained Shorty.

"Won't the mobile library come
to her?"

"Er, no," said Rails, thinking fast. "Gran's got vicious dogs. They won't let anyone in the house."

Miss Wolf stroked her chin thoughtfully. "Vicious dogs. I see," she said, "I have some experience with them."

"So, Miss, seeing she only lives around the corner, will you let Gran use the school library?" begged Rails.

"Of course I will," replied Miss Wolf. "Your grandmother will receive my every attention. It will be an honor to have her in the library."

The plan was working to perfection.

Two days later, shortly before the

library was due to close, a small, grey-haired lady hobbled into the library.

"I'm Gran Porker," she announced in a peculiar, squeaky voice.

"How charming to meet you," said Miss Wolf. "I'm—"

"I know who you are," said Gran.

"The kiddies talk about you all the time. They think the world of you. You're a real marvel, that's what they say."

"Gosh!" said Miss Wolf. "Goodness, gracious. Do they truly say that? The darlings! Oh golly gosh, that's nice!"

"You're their hero," said Gran.

"Please, stop. You'll have me crying if you don't."

"Really?" said Gran.

"Yes, indeed. I'm on the verge of an ocean of tears. One more word and—"

"Those kiddies love you!" said Gran.

"Waaahhhhh!"

Miss Wolf"s face was awash
with tears.

She cried so loudly she didn't hear
the phone ring.

Gran picked it up. Without asking
who it was, she passed the phone to
Miss Wolf.

"It's for you," she said.

SEVEN

"Meet me at the town-hall clock in ten minutes," the caller whispered in an odd voice that was almost as squeaky as Gran Porker's.

"What on earth for?" said Miss Wolf. "I don't know who you are, or what you want."

"Miss Wolf," said the mystery man, "I am your secret admirer."

"You are?"

"Yes! I love your mind. I love your eyes, your hair, and your nose."

"My nose, too?"

"Even your sticking-out ears."

"Gosh!"

"Miss Wolf . . . "

"Yes?"

"I want you to be my sweetheart!"

"You do? Oh, dearie me. In
that case, I'll be there in two minutes.
Make that thirty seconds! Don't
go away!"

"One last thing," said the caller.

"Yes, my sweet?"

"I might be a bit delayed—but
you'll wait for me, won't you?"

"Oh, I will, I will!" said Miss Wolf
passionately.

Gran looked up from the book she
was pretending to read. "Is everything
all right?"

"Goodness, look at the time," said
Miss Wolf. "I have to close up now,
I'm afraid. Could you come back
tomorrow, dear?"

"You mean I walked all this way for nothing?" Gran Porker snapped. "I almost got run over five times, I slipped on a banana, and a dog chased me. Now I'm being kicked out!"

Miss Wolf eyed her watch. Her secret admirer tugged at her mind. Yet she couldn't disappoint Gran Porker.

"Here you are, dear heart," she said, handing over a spare set of library keys. "I know I can trust you. Have a jolly good look around and then lock up. Cheerio!"

The very second the librarian was out the door, Gran Porker, who was really Rails in disguise, whipped out a heap of king-sized garbage bags from under her dress.

She whizzed down the aisles, dumping books into the bags. As each one was filled she dragged it to the bathroom and hurled it out the window, where Shorty waited.

A few moments later Dan rode up, parking his bike beside those of Shorty and Rails.

"What fun!" he cried. "Wolfie had no idea it was me pretending to be her secret admirer."

The Porkers hooted with glee.

Poor Miss Wolf was in for a big surprise.

EIGHT

The Porkers lashed the bags onto the sides of their bikes and pedalled furiously. Load after load of books disappeared with them as they sped into the bush.

Meanwhile, Miss Wolf waited patiently at the town-hall clock.

An hour crawled by, then two, then three. Then it was dark. Still no one came to meet her.

Finally she faced the truth. "What a silly sausage I am," she told herself.

"No one's going to come. I allowed my heart to be shattered by a common trickster. But who would do such a foul deed. And why?"

Miss Wolf was back at Mount Barker School early the next morning, as bright and breezy as ever.

Pinned to her chest was a badge that said: "IT TAKES MORE THAN A BROKEN HEART TO STOP A LIBRARIAN."

"Hmm," she thought as she walked inside the library. "Something seems a little bit different. I wonder what it is . . . "

She looked more closely.

"Oh, my gracious, no!"

Her mouth fell open in horror. Her jaw dropped so far down that it almost knocked over two cockroaches playing soccer on the carpet.

There was nothing but empty shelves!

"Blinketty, blinketty Bill!" she gasped. "The books! The books! They're gone!

Help! Help! Someone's stolen the library!"

Miss Wolf was a soggy bundle of tears. She was trying to decide who to call first—the Book Police, or the Royal Society for the Prevention of Cruelty to Librarians—when she noticed a lady's dress tucked under one of the shelves.

Next to it was a grey wig.

Inside the wig were little strands of curly, bright red hair.

"I smell a rat," she said aloud. "No, no, not a rat…I smell a Porker!"

Just then, Mr. Kidney stepped into the library. "Hello, Miss Wolf," he said cheerily. "Everything going well, I hope?"

Her head was bowed. "I'm stressed," she said. "I'm very, very stressed."

The ever observant Mr. Kidney noticed the missing books. "Ah, lots of borrowings today, I see. Yes, that *can* be stressful."

Miss Wolf looked up, and growled.

What Mr. Kidney saw made him shudder. As he stared, tiny Miss Wolf grew taller and stronger, until she towered over him.

There was something else, too. From head to toe, her body was covered with coarse black hair!

NINE

Mr. Kidney remained cool, as only principals can.

"I don't think you're quite yourself today," he said. "Perhaps you should have the rest of the day off."

With giant hairy hands Miss Wolf plucked him up and sat him on the Reference shelf.

"It's those Porkers," she said, her voice low and threatening. "They stole my library—and what's more, they broke my heart! No one does that to the Wolf!"

"Have a whole wwwweek off," said the no longer cool Mr. Kidney.

"Maybe I will," she hissed at him. "But first, I'll catch those beastly brats!"

Miss Wolf galloped out of the library on all fours, like a wild animal.

Behind her trailed a long and furry tail!

Once outside, Miss Wolf reared up on her hind legs and sniffed the air until she picked up the Porker trail. Then she was off, thundering along with a clompitty-clomp of her heavy paws, snarling as she ran.

Her head was huge. It had to be to contain her monstrous eyes and nose, her cavernous mouth. And what about those teeth? They were big enough to bite a shark in half!

She was no longer kind Miss Wolf. Stress had turned her into a wolf— a big, bad wolf!

TEN

The Porker children were high up in a tree when Miss Wolf tracked them down. They stood on a platform outside a treehouse they'd just finished building—a treehouse, made entirely out of library books.

"Silly old Wolfie," said Rails. "She'll never work out what happened."

"We're much too smart for the likes of her," agreed Dan.

"GGGRROWWLL!"

"There's some kind of crazy dog

down there," said Shorty.

"I think it's a wolf," said Dan. "It is! It's a giant wolf."

Rails stared and stared at the wolf. "It looks strangely familiar," she said.

The wolf leapt several feet high up into the tree, growling fiercely as it hopped from branch to branch, ever closer to the treehouse.

Before the Porkers could move, it was right in front of them.

"HELLO, CHILDREN," boomed the wolf.

Rails wasn't frightened. "This is a trick," she said. "Wolves can't talk."

"Librarian wolves can," growled

the wolf. "We can do anything when we're stressed!"

Rails gulped. "Librarian? Stress? Oh, no! It's Miss Wolf!"

"Yum, yum!" said the wolf.

"What big eyes you have," said Rails.

"All the better to see you with," snarled the wolf.

"What big teeth you have," said Dan.

"All the better to eat you with!"

"What a big bottom you have," said Shorty.

"All the better to—what did you say?"

"I said your bottom is . . ."

"No! Not another word! That was the final straw! I'm going to gobble you up!"

"Move!" yelled Rails. "Into the treehouse!"

Quick as a blink the Porkers dashed inside the treehouse.

ELEVEN

"Let me in," said the wolf, thumping at the door. "Let me in!"

"No way!"

"Then I'll huff and I'll puff and I'll blow your house down!"

"Go ahead and try, you big bag of wind," said Dan.

"*We* lined our house with big thick books, with hardly any pictures in them," added Shorty. "A cyclone wouldn't shift it."

"Watch this!" cried the wolf.

One huff and a puff was more
than enough.

WHOOSH!

Down came the treehouse, books scattered near and far. The Porkers came down, too, landing with a thump and a bump. And when they stood, the wolf pounced!

"Gotcha!" she howled.

She pinned Rails and Shorty under her massive tail. She lifted Dan above her head and opened her dribbling mouth...

"No! No!" shouted Principal Kidney, who'd followed Miss Wolf from the library.

"Go away," said the wolf. "You'll spoil my breakfast."

"It's time we had a little talk," said

the Principal.

The wolf bared her teeth, but
Mr. Kidney stood his ground.

"The Porkers probably deserve to
be eaten," he said, "but not by you,
Miss Wolf."

"Look at me! I'm a wolf! I'm
allowed to eat whoever I like!"

Mr. Kidney folded his arms. "I don't

care what you look like," he said.
"Deep down, you'll always be a
librarian. And, no matter how much
they might feel like doing it, librarians
are not allowed to eat children."

"Even when they're very, very
stressed?" asked the wolf.

"Especially then," said Mr. Kidney.

"Oh, blinketty, blinketty Bill,"
grumbled the wolf.

Then, slowly but surely, as the
Porkers watched in horrified awe,
the wolf's head became smaller. Its
whole body shrank. Its hairiness
disappeared. The last thing to go was
its tail, and then it wasn't a wolf at all.

It was simply Miss Wolf.

"Come now, children," she said when she was herself again. "You must pick up every one of these books. Quickly now. The library is waiting!"

Dan bent over in front of Rails to pick up a book.

"Aaarrgghh!" shrieked Rails.

Dan spun around, gaped at something, and also shrieked.

Suddenly, for no apparent reason, each of the Porkers cried and screamed. They wailed their wicked heads off!

"What's wrong with you?" asked Mr. Kidney.

"Look!" said Rails, swinging around to show her backside.

Dan and Shorty swung around, too.

They all had curly, piggy tails!

"I don't remember seeing them before," said Mr. Kidney, scratching his head.

"It's the stress!" moaned Rails.

"The stress has given us tails!" bellowed Dan.

"It's not fair!" squawked Shorty.

"Ah, stress," said Miss Wolf. "It does such terrible things. But never mind, children, if you're exceptionally good, the tails might disappear . . . in a year or two."

From Bill Condon

When I was at school I was a very good little boy who was never brave enough to do naughty things. At least that's what everyone thought. No one suspected that it was I who made those clucking noises that drove teachers crazy. It was I who put the plastic doggy doo on the teachers' seats. I am so glad that I never had a teacher like Miss Wolf. I would have been in BIG trouble.

From Caroline Magerl

I used to draw pictures of naked teachers in class. Imagine my bliss when I got to draw the principal's bottom for this book and I wasn't going to be sent to the principal's office. That was just one of the fun aspects of illustrating this book. For a secret schoolroom scribbler this book has the lot—bug-eating teachers, chundering children . . .